THE QUEEN'S NECKLACE

Maurice Leblanc

first published in French on April 15, 1906

translated in 1910 by Alexander Teixeira de Mattos

Two or three times each year, on occasions of unusual importance, such as the balls at the Austrian Embassy or the soirées of Lady Billingstone, the Countess de Dreux-Soubise wore upon her white shoulders "The Queen's Necklace."

It was, indeed, the famous necklace, the

legendary necklace that Bohmer and Bassenge, court jewelers, had made for Madame Du Barry; the veritable necklace that the Cardinal de Rohan-Soubise intended to give to Marie-Antoinette, Queen of France; and the same that the adventuress Jeanne de Valois, Countess de la Motte, had pulled to pieces one evening in February, 1785, with the aid of her husband and their accomplice, Rétaux de Villette.

To tell the truth, the mounting alone was genuine. Rétaux de Villette had kept it, whilst the Count de la Motte and his wife scattered to the four winds of heaven the beautiful stones so carefully chosen by Bohmer. Later, he sold the mounting to Gaston de Dreux-Soubise, nephew and heir of the Cardinal, who re-purchased the few diamonds that remained in the possession of the English jeweler, Jeffreys; supplemented them with other stones of the same size but of much inferior quality, and thus restored the marvelous necklace to the form in which it had come from the hands of Bohmer and Bassenge.

For nearly a century, the house of Dreux-Soubise had prided itself upon the possession of this historic jewel. Although adverse circumstances had greatly reduced their fortune, they preferred to curtail their household expenses rather than part with this relic of royalty. More particularly, the present count clung to it as a man clings to the home of his ancestors. As a matter of prudence, he had rented a safety-deposit box at the Crédit Lyonnais in which to keep it.

He went for it himself on the afternoon of the day on which his wife wished to wear it, and he, himself, carried it back next morning.

On this particular evening, at the reception given at the Palais de Castille, the Countess achieved a remarkable success; and King Christian, in whose honor the fête was given, commented on her grace and beauty. The thousand facets of the diamond sparkled and shone like flames of fire about her shapely neck and shoulders, and it is safe to say that none but she could have borne the weight of such an ornament with so much ease and grace.

This was a double triumph, and the Count de Dreux was highly elated when they returned to their chamber in the old house of the faubourg Saint-Germain. He was proud of his wife, and quite as proud, perhaps, of the necklace that had conferred added luster to his noble house for generations. His

wife, also, regarded
the necklace with
an almost childish
vanity, and it was
not without regret
that she removed it
from her shoulders
and handed it to her
husband who admired
it as passionately
as if he had never
seen it before. Then,
having placed it
in its case of red
leather, stamped
with the Cardinal's

arms, he passed into an adjoining room which was simply an alcove or cabinet that had been cut off from their chamber, and which could be entered only by means of a door at the foot of their bed. As he had done on previous occasions, he hid it on a high shelf amongst hat-boxes and piles of linen. He closed the door, and retired.

Next morning, he arose about nine o'clock, intending to go to the Crédit Lyonnais before breakfast. He dressed, drank a cup of coffee, and went to the stables to give his orders. The condition of one of the horses worried him. He caused it to be exercised in his presence. Then he returned to his wife, who had not yet left the chamber. Her maid was dressing her hair. When her husband entered, she asked:

"Are you going out?"

"Yes, as far as the bank."

"Of course. That is wise."

He entered the cabinet; but, after a few seconds, and without any sign of astonishment, he asked:

"Did you take it, my dear?"

"What?....No, I have not taken anything."

"You must have moved it."

"Not at all. I have not even opened that door."

He appeared at the door, disconcerted, and stammered, in a scarcely intelligible voice:

"You haven't.... It wasn't you?.... Then...."

She hastened to his assistance, and, together, they made

a thorough search, throwing the boxes to the floor and overturning the piles of linen. Then the count said, quite discouraged:

"It is useless to look any more. I put it here, on this shelf."

"You must be mistaken."

"No, no, it was on this shelf—nowhere else."

They lighted a candle, as the room was quite dark, and then carried out all the linen and other articles that the room contained. And, when the room was emptied, they confessed, in despair, that the famous necklace had disappeared. Without losing time in vain lamentations, the countess notified the commissary of police, Mon. Valorbe, who came at once, and, after hearing their story, inquired of the count:

"Are you sure that no one passed through your chamber during the night?"

"Absolutely sure, as I am a very light sleeper. Besides, the chamber door was bolted, and I remember unbolting it this morning when my wife rang for her maid."

"And there is no other entrance to the cabinet?"

"None."

"No windows?"

"Yes, but it is closed up."

"I will look at it."

Candles were lighted, and Mon. Valorbe observed at once that the lower half of the window was covered by a large press which was, however, so narrow that it did not touch the casement on either side.

"On what does this window open?"

"A small inner court."

"And you have a floor above this?"

"Two; but, on a level with the servant's floor, there is a close grating over the court. That is why this room is so dark."

When the press was moved, they found that the window

was fastened, which would not have been the case if anyone had entered that way.

"Unless," said the count, "they went out through our chamber."

"In that case, you would have found the door unbolted."

The commissary considered the

situation for a moment, then asked the countess:

"Did any of your servants know that you wore the necklace last evening?"

"Certainly; I didn't conceal the fact. But nobody knew that it was hidden in that cabinet."

"No one?"

"No one.... unless...."

"Be quite sure, madam, as it is a very important point."

She turned to her husband, and said:

"I was thinking of Henriette."

"Henriette? She didn't know where we kept it."

"Are you sure?"

"Who is this woman Henriette?" asked Mon. Valorbe.

"A school-mate, who was disowned by her family for marrying beneath her. After her husband's death, I furnished an apartment in this house for her and her son. She is clever with her needle and has done some work for me."

"What floor is she on?"

"Same as ours....
at the end of the
corridor.... and I
think.... the window
of her kitchen...."

"Opens on this little
court, does it not?"

"Yes, just opposite
ours."

Mon. Valorbe
then asked to see
Henriette. They went

to her apartment; she was sewing, whilst her son Raoul, about six years old, was sitting beside her, reading. The commissary was surprised to see the wretched apartment that had been provided for the woman. It consisted of one room without a fireplace, and a very small room that served as a kitchen.

The commissary proceeded to question her. She appeared to be overwhelmed on learning of the theft. Last evening she had herself dressed the countess and placed the necklace upon her shoulders.

"Good God!" she exclaimed, "it can't be possible!"

"And you have no idea? Not the least suspicion? Is it possible that the thief may have passed through your room?"

She laughed heartily, never supposing that she could be an object of suspicion.

"But I have not left my room. I never go out. And, perhaps, you have not seen?"

She opened the kitchen window, and said:

"See, it is at least three metres to the ledge of the opposite window."

"Who told you that we supposed the theft might have been committed in that way?"

"But.... the necklace was in the cabinet, wasn't it?"

"How do you know that?"

"Why, I have always known that it was kept there at night. It had been mentioned in my presence."

Her face, though still young, bore unmistakable traces of sorrow and resignation. And it now assumed an expression of anxiety as if some danger threatened her. She drew her son toward her. The child took her hand, and kissed it affectionately.

When they were alone again, the count said to the commissary:

"I do not suppose you suspect Henriette. I can answer for her. She is honesty itself."

"I quite agree with you," replied Mon. Valorbe. "At most, I thought there might have been an unconscious complicity. But I confess that even that theory must be abandoned, as it does not help solve the problem now before us."

The commissary of police abandoned the investigation, which was now taken up and completed by the examining judge. He questioned the servants, examined the condition of the bolt, experimented with the opening and closing of the cabinet window, and explored the little court from top to bottom. All was in vain. The bolt was intact. The window could not be opened or closed from the outside.

The inquiries especially concerned Henriette, for, in spite of everything, they always turned in her direction. They made a thorough investigation of her past life, and ascertained that, during the last three years, she had left the house only four times, and her business, on those occasions, was satisfactorily explained. As a matter of fact, she acted as chambermaid and seamstress to the countess, who treated her with great strictness and even severity.

At the end of a week, the examining judge had secured no more definite information than the commissary of police. The judge said:

"Admitting that we know the guilty party, which we do not, we are confronted by the fact that we do not know how the theft was committed. We are brought face to face with two obstacles: a door and a window—both closed and fastened. It is thus a double mystery. How could anyone enter, and, moreover, how could any one escape, leaving behind him a bolted door and a fastened window?"

At the end of four months, the secret opinion of the judge was that the count and countess, being hard pressed for money, which was their normal condition, had sold the Queen's Necklace. He closed the investigation.

The loss of the famous jewel was a severe blow to

the Dreux-Soubise. Their credit being no longer propped up by the reserve fund that such a treasure constituted, they found themselves confronted by more exacting creditors and money-lenders. They were obliged to cut down to the quick, to sell or mortgage every article that possessed any commercial value. In brief, it would have been their ruin, if two large legacies from some distant relatives had not saved them.

Their pride also suffered a downfall, as if they had lost a quartering from their escutcheon. And, strange to relate, it was upon her former schoolmate,

Henriette, that the countess vented her spleen. Toward her, the countess displayed the most spiteful feelings, and even openly accused her. First, Henriette was relegated to the servants' quarters, and, next day, discharged.

For some time, the count and countess passed an uneventful

life. They traveled a great deal. Only one incident of record occurred during that period. Some months after the departure of Henriette, the countess was surprised when she received and read the following letter, signed by Henriette:

"Madame,"

"I do not know how to thank you; for it

was you, was it not, who sent me that? It could not have been anyone else. No one but you knows where I live. If I am wrong, excuse me, and accept my sincere thanks for your past favors...."

What did the letter mean? The present or past favors of the countess consisted principally of injustice and neglect. Why, then, this letter of thanks?

When asked for an explanation, Henriette replied that she had received a letter, through the mails, enclosing two bank-notes of one thousand francs each. The envelope, which she enclosed with her reply, bore the Paris post-mark, and was addressed in a handwriting that was obviously disguised. Now, whence came those two thousand francs? Who had sent them? And why had they sent them?

Henriette received a similar letter and a like sum of money twelve months later. And a third time; and a fourth; and each year for a period of six years, with this difference, that in the fifth and sixth years the sum was doubled. There was another difference: the post-office authorities having seized one of the letters under the pretext that it was not registered, the last two letters were duly sent according to the postal regulations, the first dated from Saint-Germain, the other from Suresnes. The writer signed the first one, "Anquety"; and the other, "Péchard." The addresses that he gave were false.

At the end of six years, Henriette died, and the mystery remained unsolved.

All these events are known to the public.

The case was one of those which excite public interest, and it was a strange coincidence that this necklace, which had caused such a great commotion in France at the close of the eighteenth century, should create a similar commotion a century later. But what I am about to relate is known only to the parties directly interested and a few others from whom the count exacted a promise of secrecy. As it is probable that some day or other that promise will be broken, I have no hesitation in rending the veil and thus disclosing the key to the mystery, the explanation of the letter published in the morning papers two days ago; an extraordinary letter which increased, if possible, the mists and shadows that envelope this inscrutable drama.

Five days ago, a number of guests were dining with the Count de Dreux-Soubise. There were several ladies present, including his two nieces and his cousin, and the following gentlemen: the president of Essaville, the deputy Bochas, the chevalier Floriani, whom the count had known in Sicily, and General Marquis de Rouzières, an old club friend.

After the repast, coffee was served by the ladies, who gave the gentlemen permission to smoke their cigarettes, provided they would not desert the salon. The conversation was general, and finally one of the guests chanced to speak of celebrated crimes. And that gave the Marquis de Rouzières, who delighted to tease the count, an opportunity to mention the affair of the Queen's Necklace, a subject that the count detested.

Each one expressed his own opinion of the affair; and, of course, their various theories were not only contradictory but impossible.

"And you, monsieur," said the countess to the chevalier Floriani, "what is your opinion?"

"Oh! I—I have no opinion, madame."

All the guests protested; for the chevalier had just related in an entertaining manner various adventures in which he had participated with his father, a magistrate at Palermo, and which established his judgment and taste in such manners.

"I confess," said he, "I have sometimes succeeded in unraveling mysteries that the cleverest detectives have renounced; yet I do not claim to be Sherlock Holmes. Moreover, I know very little about the affair of the Queen's Necklace."

Everybody now turned to the

count, who was thus obliged, quite unwillingly, to narrate all the circumstances connected with the theft. The chevalier listened, reflected, asked a few questions, and said:

"It is very strange.... at first sight, the problem appears to be a very simple one."

The count shrugged his shoulders. The others drew closer to the chevalier, who continued, in a dogmatic tone:

"As a general rule, in order to find the author of a crime or a theft, it is necessary to determine how that crime or theft was committed, or, at least, how it could have been committed. In the present case, nothing is more simple, because we are face to face, not with several theories, but with one positive fact, that is to say: the thief could only enter by the chamber door or the window of the cabinet. Now, a person cannot open a bolted door from the outside.

Therefore, he must have entered through the window."

"But it was closed and fastened, and we found it fastened afterward," declared the count.

"In order to do that," continued Floriani, without heeding the interruption, "he had simply to construct a bridge, a plank or a ladder, between the balcony of the kitchen and the ledge of the window, and as the jewel-case—"

"But I repeat that the window was fastened," exclaimed the count, impatiently.

This time, Floriani was obliged to reply. He did so with the greatest tranquility, as if the objection was the most insignificant affair in the world.

"I will admit that it was; but is there not a transom in the upper part of the window?"

"How do you know that?"

"In the first place, that was customary in houses of that date; and, in the second place, without such a transom, the theft cannot be explained."

"Yes, there is one, but it was closed, the same as the window. Consequently, we did not pay attention to it."

"That was a mistake; for, if you had examined it, you would have found that it had been opened."

"But how?"

"I presume that, like all others, it opens by means of a wire with a ring on the lower end."

"Yes, but I do not see—"

"Now, through a hole in the window, a person could, by the aid of some instrument, let us say a poker with a hook at the end, grip the ring, pull down, and open the transom."

The count laughed and said:

"Excellent! excellent! Your scheme is very cleverly constructed, but you overlook one thing, monsieur, there is no hole in the window."

"There was a hole."

"Nonsense, we would have seen it."

"In order to see it, you must look for it, and no one has looked. The hole is there; it must be there, at the side of the window, in the putty. In a vertical direction, of course."

The count arose. He was greatly excited. He paced up and down the room, two or three times, in a nervous manner; then, approaching Floriani, said:

"Nobody has been in that room since; nothing has been changed."

"Very well, monsieur, you can easily satisfy yourself that my explanation is correct."

"It does not agree with the facts established by the examining judge. You have seen nothing, and yet you contradict all that we have seen and all that we know."

Floriani paid no attention to the count's petulance. He simply smiled and said:

"Mon Dieu, monsieur, I submit my theory; that is all. If I am mistaken, you can easily prove it."

"I will do so at once....I confess that your assurance—"

The count muttered a few more words; then suddenly rushed to the door and passed out. Not a word was uttered in his absence; and this profound silence gave the situation an air of almost tragic importance. Finally, the count returned. He was pale and nervous. He said to his friends, in a trembling voice:

"I beg your pardon..... the revelations of the chevalier were so unexpected.....I should never have thought....."

His wife questioned him, eagerly:

"Speak.... what is it?"

He stammered: "The hole is there, at the very spot, at the side of the window—"

He seized the chevalier's arm, and said to him in an imperious tone:

"Now, monsieur, proceed. I admit that you are right so far,

but now.... that is not all.... go on.... tell us the rest of it."

Floriani disengaged his arm gently, and, after a moment, continued:

"Well, in my opinion, this is what happened. The thief, knowing that the countess was going to wear the necklace that evening, had prepared his gangway or bridge during your absence. He watched you through the window and saw you hide the necklace. Afterward, he cut the glass and pulled the ring."

"Ah! but the distance was so great that it would be impossible for him to reach the window-fastening through the transom."

"Well, then, if he could not open the window by reaching through the transom, he must have crawled through the transom."

"Impossible; it is too small. No man could crawl through it."

"Then it was not a man," declared Floriani.

"What!"

"If the transom is too small to admit a man, it must have been a child."

"A child!"

"Did you not say that your friend Henriette had a son?"

"Yes; a son named Raoul."

"Then, in all probability, it was Raoul who committed the theft."

"What proof have you of that?"

"What proof! Plenty of it....For instance—"

He stopped, and reflected for a moment, then continued:

"For instance, that gangway or bridge. It is improbable that the child could have brought it in from outside the house and carried it away again without being observed. He must have used something close at hand. In the little room used by Henriette as a kitchen, were there not some shelves against the wall on which she placed her pans and dishes?"

"Two shelves, to the best of my memory."

"Are you sure that those shelves are really fastened to the wooden brackets that support them? For, if they are not, we could be justified in presuming that the child removed them, fastened them together, and thus formed his bridge. Perhaps, also, since there was a stove, we might find the bent poker that he used to open the transom."

Without saying a word, the count left the room; and, this time, those present did not feel the nervous anxiety they had experienced the first time. They were confident that Floriani was right, and no one was surprised when the count returned and declared:

"It was the child. Everything proves it."

"You have seen the shelves and the poker?"

"Yes. The shelves have been unnailed, and the poker is there yet."

But the countess exclaimed:

"You had better say it was his mother.

Henriette is the guilty party. She must have compelled her son—"

"No," declared the chevalier, "the mother had nothing to do with it."

"Nonsense! they occupied the same room. The child could not have done it without the mother's knowledge."

"True, they lived in the same room, but all this happened in the adjoining room, during the night, while the mother was asleep."

"And the necklace?" said the count. "It would have been found amongst the child's things."

"Pardon me! He had been out. That morning, on which

you found him reading, he had just come from school, and perhaps the commissary of police, instead of wasting his time on the innocent mother, would have been better employed in searching the child's desk amongst his school-books."

"But how do you explain those two thousand francs that

Henriette received each year? Are they not evidence of her complicity?"

"If she had been an accomplice, would she have thanked you for that money? And then, was she not closely watched? But the child, being free, could easily go to a neighboring city, negotiate with some dealer and sell him one diamond or two diamonds, as he might wish, upon condition that the money should be sent from Paris, and that proceeding could be repeated from year to year."

An indescribable anxiety oppressed the Dreux-Soubise and their guests. There was something in the tone and attitude of Floriani— something more than the chevalier's assurance which, from the beginning, had so annoyed the count. There was a touch of irony, that seemed rather hostile than sympathetic. But the count affected to laugh, as he said:

"All that is very ingenious and

interesting, and I congratulate you upon your vivid imagination."

"No, not at all," replied Floriani, with the utmost gravity, "I imagine nothing. I simply describe the events as they must have occurred."

"But what do you know about them?"

"What you yourself have told me. I picture to myself the life of the mother and child down there in the country; the illness of the mother, the schemes of and inventions of the child to sell the precious stones in order to save his mother's life, or, at least, soothe her dying moments. Her illness overcomes her. She dies. Years roll on. The child becomes a man; and then—and now I will give my imagination a free rein—let us suppose that the man feels a desire to return to the home of his childhood, that he does so, and that he meets there certain people who suspect and accuse his mother.... do you realize the sorrow and anguish of such an interview in the very house wherein the original drama was played?"

His words seemed to echo for a few seconds in the ensuing silence, and one could read upon the faces of the Count and Countess de Dreux a bewildered effort to comprehend his meaning and, at the same time, the fear and anguish of such a comprehension. The count spoke at last, and said:

"Who are you, monsieur?"

"I? The chevalier Floriani, whom you met at Palermo, and whom you have been gracious enough to invite to your house on several occasions."

"Then what does this story mean?"

"Oh! nothing at all! It is simply a pastime, so far as I am concerned. I endeavor to depict the pleasure that Henriette's son, if he still lives, would have in telling you that he was the guilty party, and that he did it because his mother was unhappy, as she was on the point of losing the place of a.... servant, by which she lived, and because the child suffered at sight of his mother's sorrow."

He spoke with suppressed emotion, rose partially and inclined toward the countess. There could be no doubt that the chevalier Floriani was Henriette's son. His attitude and words proclaimed it. Besides, was it not his obvious intention and desire to be recognized as such?

The count hesitated. What action would he take against the audacious guest? Ring? Provoke a scandal? Unmask the man who had once robbed him? But that was a long time ago! And who would believe that absurd story about the guilty child? No; better far to accept the situation, and pretend not to comprehend the true meaning of it. So the count, turning to Floriani, exclaimed:

"Your story is very curious, very

entertaining; I enjoyed it much. But what do you think has become of this young man, this model son? I hope he has not abandoned the career in which he made such a brilliant début."

"Oh! certainly not."

"After such a début! To steal the Queen's Necklace at six years of age; the celebrated necklace that was coveted by Marie-Antoinette!"

"And to steal it," remarked Floriani, falling in with the count's mood, "without costing him the slightest trouble, without anyone thinking to examine the condition of the window, or to observe that the window-sill was too clean—that window-sill which he had wiped in order to efface the marks he had made in the thick dust. We must admit that it was sufficient to turn the head of a boy at that age. It was all so easy. He had simply to desire the thing, and reach out his hand to get it."

"And he reached out his hand."

"Both hands," replied the chevalier, laughing.

His companions received a shock. What mystery surrounded the life of the so-called Floriani? How wonderful must have been the life of that adventurer, a thief at six years of age, and who, to-day, in search of excitement or, at most, to gratify a feeling of resentment, had come to brave his victim in her own house, audaciously, foolishly, and yet with all the grace and delicacy of a courteous guest!

He arose and approached the countess to bid her

adieu. She recoiled, unconsciously. He smiled.

"Oh! Madame, you are afraid of me! Did I pursue my role of parlor-magician a step too far?"

She controlled herself, and replied, with her accustomed ease:

"Not at all, monsieur. The legend of that

dutiful son interested me very much, and I am pleased to know that my necklace had such a brilliant destiny. But do you not think that the son of that woman, that Henriette, was the victim of hereditary influence in the choice of his vocation?"

He shuddered, feeling the point, and replied:

"I am sure of it; and, moreover, his natural tendency to crime must have been very strong or he would have been discouraged."

"Why so?"

"Because, as you must know, the majority of the diamonds were false.

The only genuine stones were the few purchased from the English jeweler, the others having been sold, one by one, to meet the cruel necessities of life."

"It was still the Queen's Necklace, monsieur," replied the countess, haughtily, "and that is something that he,

Henriette's son, could not appreciate."

"He was able to appreciate, madame, that, whether true or false, the necklace was nothing more that an object of parade, an emblem of senseless pride."

The count made a threatening gesture, but his wife stopped him.

"Monsieur," she said, "if the man to whom you allude has the slightest sense of honor—"

She stopped, intimidated by Floriani's cool manner.

"If that man has the slightest sense of honor," he repeated.

She felt that she would not gain

anything by speaking to him in that manner, and in spite of her anger and indignation, trembling as she was from humiliated pride, she said to him, almost politely:

"Monsieur, the legend says that Rétaux de Villette, when in possession of the Queen's Necklace, did not disfigure the mounting. He understood that the diamonds were simply the ornament, the accessory, and that the mounting was the essential work, the creation of the artist, and he respected it accordingly. Do you think that this man had the same feeling?"

"I have no doubt that the mounting still exists. The child respected it."

"Well, monsieur, if you should happen to meet him, will you tell him that he unjustly keeps possession of a relic that is the property and pride of a certain family, and that, although the stones have been removed, the Queen's necklace still belongs to the house of Dreux-Soubise. It belongs to us as much as our name or our honor."

The chevalier replied, simply:

"I shall tell him, madame."

He bowed to her, saluted the count and the other guests, and departed.

Four days later, the countess de Dreux found upon the table in her chamber a red leather case bearing the cardinal's arms. She opened it, and found the Queen's Necklace.

But as all things must, in the life of a man who strives for unity and logic, converge toward the same goal—and as a little advertising never does any harm—on the following day, the 'Echo de France' published these sensational lines:

"The Queen's Necklace, the famous historical jewelry stolen from the family of Dreux-Soubise, has been recovered by Arsène Lupin, who hastened to restore it to its rightful owner. We cannot too highly commend such a delicate and chivalrous act."

ABOUT THE AUTHOR

Maurice Leblanc dropped out of law school to become a writer and move to Paris. His early works were critically acclaimed but had little commercial success. It is believed an editor asked him to write a French response to Sherlock Holmes and the instantly popular gentlemen thief Arsène Lupin was born.

ABOUT THE COVER

The image on the cover is adapted from the book cover from the 1910 french edition of "Arsène Lupin contre Herlock Sholmès".

MORE BOOKS AT:

superlargeprint.com

KEEP ON READING!

ISBN 9798748190138

Printed in Great Britain
by Amazon

70650205R00068